N___ all,
you be
safe
happy
& filled with love.

Michi L

MAY ALL PEOPLE and Pigs BE HAPPY

MICKI FINE PAVLICEK

Illustrated by John Pavlicek

North Atlantic Books
Berkeley, California

Published by
North Atlantic Books
Berkeley, California

Printed in China

Cover art and interior illustrations by John Pavlicek
Cover design by Jasmine Hromjak
Book design by Happenstance Type-O-Rama

May All People and Pigs Be Happy is sponsored and published by the Society for the Study of Native Arts and Sciences (dba North Atlantic Books), an educational nonprofit based in Berkeley, California, that collaborates with partners to develop cross-cultural perspectives, nurture holistic views of art, science, the humanities, and healing, and seed personal and global transformation by publishing work on the relationship of body, spirit, and nature.

North Atlantic Books' publications are available through most bookstores. For further information, visit our website at www.northatlanticbooks.com or call 800-733-3000.

Library of Congress Cataloguing-in-Publication data is available from the publisher upon request.

Printed and bound by Qualibre (NJ)/PrintPlus, April 2019, in China, Q-190616

1 2 3 4 5 6 7 8 9 Qualibre/PrintPlus 24 23 22 21 20 19

North Atlantic Books is committed to the protection of our environment. We print on recycled paper whenever possible and partner with printers who strive to use environmentally responsible practices.

Pigalina was Claire's soft, fuzzy pink pig. Everyone who saw Pigalina thought she was the cutest pig ever.

Claire and Pigalina did everything together.

Wherever Claire went, Pigalina went too.

One day, Claire's friend Molly got angry and called Claire a bad name. Then Molly turned her back and walked away.

Claire suddenly felt small and lonely.

She got prickly, hot tears in her eyes.

She walked home under a cloud
of sadness.

Claire grabbed Pigalina, threw herself on her bed, and cried herself to sleep.

When Claire woke up, she felt a soft fuzziness on her ear, and heard these words:

*"May you be safe.
May you be happy.
May you feel love."*

She opened her eyes. "What's wrong?" Pigalina asked.

"I'm sad about what happened with Molly, and I'm mad at her, too," Claire said.

"It's ok to feel that way. I wonder . . . maybe we could try something. . . ."

"Put your hand on your heart and the other one on your tummy."

Claire did. Then Pigalina said, "Can you feel the breath in your chest and tummy as you breathe in and out?"

Claire nodded. She felt her tummy go in and out, in and out, lots of times. It felt like Pigalina's pink fuzziness— soft and comfy.

Claire sat quietly for a while, feeling her tummy go in and out. Pigalina sat right by her side. Then Pigalina said, "Now you can say loving wishes for yourself. Say them with me:

> *May I be safe. May I be happy. May I feel love.*
> *May I be safe. May I be happy. May I feel love.*
> *May I be safe. May I be happy. May I feel love."*

They whispered the wishes again and again.

Claire whispered the wishes to herself that night.
She felt warm and peaceful in her tummy and heart.

When Claire watched her parents smiling at each other, she felt the same way as when she repeated the wishes for herself. She pulled Pigalina close.

Pigalina whispered, "Let's share our wishes with your parents." Together they softly said:

"May YOU be safe.
May you be happy.
May you feel love."

Claire silently repeated the wishes, first for herself and then for her parents. She felt even happier and safer.

When Claire and Pigalina played together, they often sent the wishes to each other:

"May WE be safe.
May we be happy.
May we feel love."

One day Claire and Pigalina saw an old man looking lonely and sad—the way Claire had felt when Molly had gotten mad at her. Claire said, "Let's send him the loving wishes, too."

So, as they walked by, they silently said to him:

> *"May YOU be safe.*
> *May you be happy.*
> *May you feel love."*

Claire hadn't known that she could love someone she didn't know.

Then, as Claire and Pigalina were crossing the street, an angry driver honked loudly at them.

At first, Claire was scared by the honk and mad at the honker.
But then she looked at Pigalina and knew what to do.
She said the wishes for herself first and then for the driver:

"May YOU be safe.
May you be happy.
May you feel love."

When they got home Pigalina said, "Even though you felt angry earlier, you sent the honker loving wishes. Maybe you could send Molly those wishes, too."

"But I'm really angry at Molly. She hurt my feelings." Claire said.

Pigalina said softly, "Yes, I know."

Claire frowned. She agreed to try it, but only if Pigalina would say the wishes with her.

So, thinking of Molly, they said:

*"May YOU be safe.
May you be happy.
May you feel love."*

After a while Claire felt safe and tender inside.

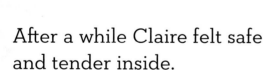

Then she said to Pigalina, "Hey, maybe we could send loving wishes to everyone in my class."

So they did.

Then they sent the wishes to Claire's whole school.

She sent the wishes to Molly and her schoolmates again that night.

The next morning, Claire woke up
full of excitement.

"Pigalina, I had a dream!"

"You and I flew around the world and dropped love blossoms on the whole world. All the people *and* all the pigs!"

Pigalina smiled. She said, "Even though we don't have a plane, we can send warm wishes to every person and every pig on Earth right now."

Together they whispered,

"May all people and pigs be safe.
May all people and pigs be happy.
May all people and pigs feel love."

Claire felt warm and happy deep, deep in her heart.

Now **you** can send loving wishes, too. First, start with yourself:

*"May I be safe.
May I be happy.
May I feel love."*

Now say these wishes for everyone:

> *"May all people and creatures be safe.*
> *May all people and creatures be happy.*
> *May all people and creatures feel love."*

Today and every day, may you offer loving wishes to yourself and all creatures of the world.

May there be love all around the world.

Dear Kids, Parents, and Educators,

We hope you like the ways of offering love to yourself and others that Claire and Pigalina have shown you. You can make a gift to yourself of loving wishes any time. When you're happy, scared, sad or mad, these wishes can help you rest in love just like Claire did. We invite you to give yourself and others loving wishes every day!

May you be safe.
May you be happy.
May you feel love.

Micki Fine Pavlicek
and
John Pavlicek

ABOUT THE AUTHOR

MICKI FINE PAVLICEK is a longtime psycho-therapist in private practice, a certified teacher of mindfulness meditation trained at the Center for Mindfulness at the University of Massachusetts, a TEDx presenter, the founder of Mindful Living (livingmindfully.org), and the author of *The Need to Please: Mindfulness Skills to Gain Freedom from People Pleasing and Approval Seeking*. She has taught mindfulness-based stress reduction and loving-kindness meditation since 1994 in a variety of settings, including her private practice, research environments, Rice University, the University of Texas MD Anderson Cancer Center, and the Jung Center.

ABOUT THE ILLUSTRATOR

JOHN PAVLICEK has worked as an illustrator, graphic designer, and artist since 1972. His paintings have been represented by Gremillion & Co., Fine Art in Houston, Texas, since 1983. Illustrating this book has deepened his respect and admiration for the masterful, professional illustrators and cartoonists past and present.